D1545775

VOLUME 3

Silly Nomads®

Jubilee Bike Race Heroes

By M. E. Mohalland and J. L. Lewis
Illustrated by Kate Santee

MOHALLAND LEWIS LLC

Published in the United States by
Mohalland Lewis, LLC

Book Design by Jon Marken
Cover art by Kate Santee

ISBN 978-0-9897106-8-8

Silly Nomads
Jubilee Bike Race Heroes

CONTENTS

Chapter One — Blast Off! 7

Chapter Two — Flyin' Bike 19

Chapter Three — Flyin' Bike — Take Two 33

Chapter Four — What Can a Dollar Buy? 45

Chapter Five — Bottles and Cans 63

Chapter Six — Junk Yard Disaster 77

Chapter Seven — Mr. Wheeler's Donkey Cart 87

Chapter Eight — The Final Lap 99

Patois Words and Phrases 111

CHAPTER 1

Blast Off!

"ressure."

"Check."

"Oxygen."

"Check."

"Landing gear."

"Check."

"Wrenches."

"CHECK!" Suhcrom huffed. "Check, check, check, check."

"A weh yu a give me alla dem checks fa?"

"All of those things you're about to say, I've already checked them," said Suhcrom. He tugged on Naddih's cape. "Start the engine!"

"Flotation device," Naddih giggled.

Suhcrom roared with laughter. "Flotation device? You might as well say Space Ghost."

"What?"

"Can't you hear it? *Space Ghost* is on," Suhcrom said, staring at the television.

He loved watching cartoons—*He-Man and the Masters of the Universe, Thundercats, Superman and His Amazing Friends*—but *Space Ghost* was his favorite because of the way he sent out electromagnetic rays from his wristbands to freeze and destroy his enemies. Suhcrom wanted to be just like him, so he had made himself wrist bands out of empty toilet paper rolls. By cutting the rolls open lengthwise, he could wrap one around each wrist and then secure them with duct tape. He felt as if he had the power to do anything whenever he had his magic wrist bands on!

"Man, forget about him," said Naddih. "Is it a check or not?"

"Yes. It's a check."

Naddih continued with his long list of system reviews—from seat belts to suction, screwdrivers to water hoses, and tires to *bully beef* sandwiches. Suhcrom was just about to abandon their imaginary spaceship when Naddih finally gave the signal.

"I'm ready now. Let's go!" Naddih adjusted his goggles and straightened his cape. They shouted together as they started their countdown.

"Ten...Nine...Eight...Seven...Six...Five...Four... Three...Two...One...BLAST-OFF!"

"*ROOOOOOAAARRR,*" they both growled loudly,

leaning backwards on the couch that had been transformed into a makeshift spacecraft.

"Holy Moly, we are going to outer space!" shouted Suhcrom.

"Don't forget about the Milky Waaaaaaaay... oh no, Suhcrom...turbulence. Turbulence! We have turbulence!"

"How can we have turbulence already, man? We just took off. Let's have turbulence later."

"Mi a di pilot, so wi a go av turbulence now."

"Okay, Mr. Space Man, but just a tiny bit."

"It's nature, man. We can't control nature."

Bumpety-bump-bump. Bumpety-bump-bump.

"Ease up on the turbulence," Suhcrom yelled. He tapped Naddih on the back of his shoulder. "I said ease up, man."

The boys bounced up and down, rocking their bodies back and forth. Suhcrom stood up on the couch, waving his arms wildly in the air. "Woo-hoo!" he shouted. He paused to listen to the questions at the end of the cartoon. "Jupiter...Jupiter is the largest planet."

"Man, sit down before the g-force gets you."

"Oh wait, I know this one, Naddih. Venus...the answer is Venus."

"Man, sit...before you lose your head."

"This is an easy one. I know this. MURRR-currrr-reeeeee!"

Rrrrrrrrrip! The cloth covering the underside of the couch suddenly split wide open and Suhcrom plunged deep inside. His foot wedged in the springs.

"OUCH!"

Naddih swung his head around as soon as he heard the horrible sound. "Holy Macaroni!" He gasped at the huge hole in the couch and at Suhcrom, who had been swallowed up inside of it.

"Yu done mash-up wi gud spaceship. Wi dead now!"

"Just don't tell Jomfeh and everything will be okay." Suhcrom wiggled and pulled on his leg, but he couldn't get his foot free.

"Oh no, Suhcrom. System failure. *Bzzzz-bzzzz.* Alert, alert. System failure!"

"Naddih, I'm stuck. Help me out of here."

"Hold on, hold on. Hole in the spaceship. Hole in the spaceship. We're losing pressure. Get ready for a crash landing!"

"There's no time to crash land no spaceship."

"Suhcrom, grab the flotation devices."

"Man, stop your nonsense. Help me get my foot out of the springs!"

Just then they heard a *knock-knock-knock.* Naddih

jumped off the couch and slowly tiptoed over to the front door.

"Shhh...wait. Don't move, Suhcrom."

"Don't move? I can't move. My foot is stuck."

"Just hold on, man. Let me see who's out there."

Knock-knock-knock. The door rattled one more time.

"Nobody's home," Naddih said in a squeaky little voice.

The voice on the other side of the door responded. "Who are you talking to?"

"You."

"Is this Naddih?"

"No, it's Jomfeh, the adult in the house, father of Suhcrom and Naddih."

"You don't sound like a grown-up."

Naddih deepened his voice. "I repeat, this is Jomfeh, Suhcrom and Naddih's father from 914 Palmerston Close, and we are not interested in anything you are selling. Thanks sincerely. Have a blessed day."

Naddih heard giggles coming from the other side of the door and became curious. He leaned down to peek through the keyhole.

"Is that your eyeball lookin' at me, Rodney?"

"Uh-huh. How did you know?"

"It's twitchin' again, Rodney. Your eyeball's twitching."

"Open the door."

"You're way too early."

"Just open the door, man. I don't want anybody to see me."

"Wait, Naddih, wait," Suhcrom yelled. "Let me get out of here first."

"Rodney can't wait. People might see him," Naddih said as he opened the door. He pulled his Superman watch out of his pocket, the one he had found in his back yard while digging for treasures, and tapped on the crystal. "You're early, man. You weren't supposed to be here until the big hand is on his right toe."

Rodney glanced at the watch. "How can you tell? He's wearing shoes."

"*Dats not di point. Yu early.*"

"I know, I know. But if I never left the house, I would be planting *callaloo* seeds," Rodney said as he chewed on a plantain and egg sandwich.

Naddih got a whiff of the sandwich. "Mmm, that smells good!"

"What happened here?" asked Rodney as he looked around the room. "It looks like a hurricane destroyed your house."

"Well...."

"Why are you wearing that silly towel around your neck?"

"You see, Rodney...."

"And what is Suhcrom doing inside the couch?"

"Well, Mr. Blabbermouth, if you would let me finish what I'm...."

"What is going on in here? Are you guys on one of your adventures again?"

"Never mind," said Suhcrom. He waved his hand at Rodney. "Just help me get out of here."

"Naddih, help me," said Rodney. "You take one arm and I'll take the other."

"Ahhh, stop...stop! Don't tug on me so hard, man," Suhcrom grumbled. "You're going to break all the bones in my body."

"See, if you had listened to me, the g-force wouldn't have gotten you," laughed Naddih.

Naddih and Rodney pulled and tugged, and tugged and pulled. Finally, after several attempts, Suhcrom wiggled his foot out of the springs and climbed out of the couch. His ankle was bruised and a little swollen but he could still walk on it.

"I'm thirsty," said Rodney.

"*Yah mon*, you must be. Look how big that sandwich is," said Suhcrom.

"Can I have some ice water to wash it down?"

"We don't have ice water," replied Naddih. "But I can get you an ice cube."

"Ice cube?"

"Yes, we only have ice cubes," said Suhcrom. "The plumbers turned off our water pipe yesterday."

"And they told us we won't have drinking water for thirty-four hours," added Naddih.

"The men never said that. They said twenty-four hours, like twenty-four hours in one day."

"Anyway, Rodney, we forgot to put water in the fridge so we only have ice cubes. Do you want one?" asked Naddih.

"Man, what am I going to do with one ice cube?"

"Suck on it," Suhcrom laughed. "Eventually it will turn into water."

"So where's Sterlin?" asked Naddih.

"He'll be here soon. He's eating breakfast." Rodney paused as he gulped down another bite of his sandwich. *Cough-cough.* "I'll take that ice cube now."

Just then, Naddih heard the secret knock. It had to be Sterlin. He quickly opened the door.

"You guys ready?" Sterlin asked. "Did you borrow the bike?"

"Yes, we've got Nigel's bike," Suhcrom said.

"Do we have any plywood?" Sterlin wondered.

"Don't worry," Naddih said. "There is a whole bunch of it at the Hart Academy."

"What about food? Do you have any food we can take?" Rodney asked, rubbing his belly.

Suhcrom laughed. "Man, you just had fried dumplin' and eggs."

"No, I didn't have dumplin' and eggs. I had a plantain and egg sandwich...you know, with hard dough bread. Dumplin' sounds really good, though."

"The point is, Rodney, you're always eating."

"Don't worry," said Naddih, patting Rodney's shoulder reassuringly. "Jomfeh went food shopping yesterday. We'll take some *bulla cake* with us."

"Okay, guys, we better hurry. If we're still here when Enomih wakes up, she will give us chores to do," said Suhcrom.

"Let's go...*gulp*...*gulp*...uh-oh."

"What is it now, Rodney?" asked Suhcrom.

"I swallowed the ice."

"Well, don't worry. It will turn to water inside your belly, ha-ha!" Suhcrom joked.

Full of energy, the four comrades gathered what they needed for their adventure. Sterlin wheeled the bike outside. Naddih tightened the cape around his neck and gave his pants a tug. Rodney took the last bite of his sandwich and grabbed a *bulla cake.*

Suhcrom turned the television off and wrote a quick note to his sister, Enomih. *Hart Academy. Bike Flyin'. Back Later.* Then he wrapped his homemade magic bands around his wrists and quickly secured them with tape as they all ran out the door.

"We're going flyin' today!" he shouted.

CHAPTER 2

Flyin' Bike

The boys were really excited as they skipped through the yard into the streets of Palmerston Close. They had been lucky to escape the house before Enomih awakened, and with both of their fathers at work until evening, they were ready to play all day long.

It was still early and the coolness of the air brushed across their cheeks as the sun quietly peeked over the horizon. Some of their neighbors were sitting out on their verandas, sipping on Jamaican coffee, reading the day's edition of *The Gleaner,* catching up on the latest news. The boys smiled and waved to Miss Velma as they passed by. They all thought she was a nice lady, but like all of the grown-ups in their neighborhood, she kept her eye on them. The boys knew if they got into too much mischief she would report it to their fathers, and then there would be consequences to pay.

For the past five years, Suhcrom and Naddih had lived here in Palmerston Close, a small community within the town of Portsmouth, Jamaica. They moved here with their mother, who was now working in America; their father, whom they affectionately called "Jomfeh"; and their sister, Enomih. Quickly they became friends with Sterlin and his younger brother, Rodney. They had been close friends ever since, like brothers, and bike flying was one of their favorite things to do.

Sterlin was the oldest of the four. His friends had given him the nickname "Spider" because he could climb just about anything. He could get up and down a coconut tree faster than lightning. No one had ever been able to break his record.

Suhcrom, age ten, was a year younger than Sterlin. He was by far the fastest runner in the group. Although the other three tried, none of them could dash out ahead of him. Whenever he ran a race at school, though, he got so nervous that he lost speed and usually came in second place. Then one day, when he raced against the boy who always came in first, Suhcrom beat him! He was so excited that, from that time forward, he referred to himself as "Cheetah."

Naddih was two years younger than Suhcrom. He loved the water and could swim like a fish from an early age. Any time someone suggested going to the beach, he was ready. It was thrilling to splash in the salty waves, and diving was even more exhilarating. This had earned him the nickname of "Dolphin" among his friends.

Rodney, the littlest one in the group, was seven, a year younger than Naddih. He was a bit sensitive, not just because of his size, but because he had a lazy eye. It was a well-known fact that Rodney's eye twitched like crazy whenever he was nervous or up to something mischievous. Even though some of the kids picked on him, he didn't care. He had a unique ability to see things that others were not able to see. One day Sterlin's cat, Stanky Spanky, went missing and Rodney had a vision that the cat was in the swamp. The boys later found the cat hiding out in the bamboo marsh where Hamburg's dog, Sticky Fingers, had chased him. The two animals were mortal enemies! The boys' mother was very happy to hear the cat was found unharmed, and from that time forward, she endearingly called Rodney her *"Likkle Wash-belly."*

These four lads spent nearly every day together going on one sort of escapade or another. However, their travels were never without some mishaps along the way. No matter what they did, things never turned out exactly as they had planned—like the time they set out to meet with a local fisherman who had caught a big sea turtle....

❨

...It happened last summer. Their friend, Mikal, was on the little island just offshore when one of the local fisherman caught a sea turtle. It took eight people to haul it in. Mikal saw it with his own eyes. It was HUGE. Mikal told a boy from the neighborhood about it, who then returned to town and told all of the townspeople. "You've got to see this turtle," he shouted to everyone. "It's the most magnificent thing I have ever seen in my whole life! And we're going to eat turtle meat—LOTS of it!" The boy was so excited he told every kid in town and Sterlin was there to hear it firsthand. Sterlin ran into Naddih and told him, and then Naddih rushed home as fast as he could to tell Suhcrom.

"Suhcrom, Suhcrom," he gasped, barely able to breathe. "Fisherman...on the island...caught the biggest turtle ever. No other Jamaican has EVER caught a turtle this big. Holy Smackaroni, Suhcrom. It's gigantic!"

"Slow down, man. You're talking too fast. What fisherman? What turtle?"

"The fisherman, you know him, the one with the dreadlocks. He caught it. Sterlin told me. And I'm going to the island with him and Rodney to eat turtle meat. Do you know how good turtle meat is?"

"Have you ever had turtle meat?"

"No, but I hear it's good. Are you going to go with us? There is enough turtle meat for an entire army to share!"

"How are we going to get there? We need a boat."

"Mikal is there right now, and Sterlin said Mikal would send the boat over for us."

"Are you sure?"

"Yes, one of the kids in the neighborhood told Sterlin. He said Mikal will send the boat."

Just then Naddih heard the secret knock at the door. "That must be Sterlin and Rodney. Let's go, Suhcrom, let's go."

"Okay, okay. Let me put my shorts on."

The four boys took off running as fast as they could. Quickly a foot race between them ensued. Suhcrom was in the lead, Sterlin and Naddih were head to head on Suhcrom's heels, but Rodney lagged way behind.

"Wait for me! Wait for me!" he called out desperately.

Finally, Rodney caught up to the others once they all reached the shore. They moved slowly down the embankment, being careful not to tumble or slip on the damp rocks and pebbles.

When they reached the edge of the cloudy, deep water, they stopped. Waving their arms, they shouted at the top of their lungs for Mikal to send the boat across the channel.

"*Mikal, wi deh yah,*" Sterlin hollered.

"Send the boat, man," Naddih called out.

"Come on, man, push it over," Sterlin yelled again. "Over here. Hurry up."

Mikal gave the boat a good shove, but the current pulled it to the left. Luckily, the boat was tied to a very long rope, so he hauled it back in and gave it another shove towards his friends. Once again it drifted to the left, so he tried a third time. This time the boat went much further, yet still not close enough.

Sterlin didn't want to wait any longer. He rolled up his pant legs and walked cautiously into the water. He stopped when the water had come up to his knees, but he couldn't quite reach the boat. So he went out a little farther. The water was getting deeper, now at his waist. He stretched out his arm, grabbed the edge of the boat, and tugged it back to shore, where Suhcrom, Naddih, and Rodney were anxiously waiting. Eagerly, they all piled in. No sooner were they on their way when Rodney shrieked.

"*AAAAAAH!!* What is that? Guys, is that a shark? SHARK!"

Naddih panicked and dove over the side of the boat.

"Man overboard! Man overboard!" shouted Rodney.

Sterlin and Suhcrom looked at each other, their eyes wide as saucers.

"I'm not hanging around for no shark to eat me alive," said Sterlin.

Before Rodney could blink an eye, Sterlin and Suhcrom jumped into the water and began paddling back to shore at record speed.

"Guys, don't leave me!" Rodney cried. And then, he jumped into the water, too. *Splash!*

As they all dragged themselves safely back to land, they shuddered at the thought of being torn apart, limb by limb, by a hungry, razor-toothed monster. They were drenched and plastered with murky black mud from head to toe, and they smelled like a pile of fish. Realizing they were safe, they all burst into nervous laughter.

Mikal watched from the island, shaking his head, finding humor at the funny scene unfolding across the way.

"What are you guys doing?" he shouted.

"We saw a shark," Rodney hollered back.

"A shark? And you jumped in the water?" Mikal yelled.

"Rodney, you're the only one who saw the shark," Suhcrom muttered.

"And what's with the 'man overboard' thing?" Naddih laughed.

"That's what they always say on TV when somebody falls off a ship."

"Why did we jump into the water if there was a shark?" Sterlin wondered.

"Yah mon, wi fool-fool eeh," Suhcrom exclaimed.

"Can we get back into the boat now?" Rodney asked.

"No, Rodney, we're going home," said Sterlin.

"Besides, the boat is downstream now," Suhcrom sighed. He watched as the boat drifted farther and farther away from them.

"But what about the turtle meat?" Rodney whined. He sniffled and started to cry.

"It's okay, Rodney. One day we will catch our own turtle," said Naddih.

Chuckling about the "shark attack" and their failed trip to the island to eat turtle meat, the boys had gone home, looking forward to their next adventure....

The morning came alive as the boys rambled through the streets, ready for a day filled with excitement. The smell of fried eggs and dumplin' filled the air. Whiffs of fried plantain and ackee and salt fish were mixed in, too. They heard the *chirp-chirp-chirping* of the birds as they made their way toward the soccer field at the edge of town, the familiar field surrounded by a chain link fence with a massive gate. Once through the gate, they would cross the field to the Hart Academy, where they planned to set up their ramp. They had all done bike flying in the street by their houses before, but rarely in the soccer field, and never on the hill by the Hart Academy. Suhcrom and Naddih knew a lot about this hill. It was where they had pitched their tent during their secret nomad adventure. Flying bikes there would be a whole new adventure!

The four lads had just reached the corner of Palmerston Close and Palmerston Way, the street that led to the massive gate, when suddenly they heard a voice call out.

"Hey guys!" It was Desreen, one of Naddih's friends from school. She was playing in her yard with a friend when the boys passed by. "What kind of trouble are you guys getting into now?"

"We're going to fly bikes," Naddih said. A wide grin spread across his face as he waved to Desreen.

"Are girls allowed to come?" she asked.

"Sure," said Naddih. "Girls can come — as long as they're not our sisters!"

Desreen was well known in the neighborhood as one of the fastest bike riders around. That girl could fly! She could beat all of the other girls, and more than half the boys, who lived there.

"Come on, Muffet. It's okay. They're my good friends."

Desreen motioned for her friend to come along. There was nothing better than bike flying...and going with the boys made it even more exciting!

"I can bring my bike," she offered.

"You don't need to bring your bike," answered Naddih. "Look, we have Nigel's super bike. It's nothing like the Jamaican Jet Street Racer, but it comes close."

"Naddih, it's not even close to the Jet Street Racer," said Suhcrom.

"Yeh, it's not as pretty and it's not as fast," Rodney chimed in.

"Maybe, but it has a lot of really cool gadgets!"

"What's that hose hanging off the back fender?" asked Desreen.

"It's to shoot out water or grease if we are being chased by bad guys."

"What about that metal box in the front?"

"That's for ice to cool sodas and drinks if you are going somewhere hot...like the desert."

"Well, we're never going to be in Egypt," laughed Rodney. *"So dat no gud fi notin."*

"Naddih, you sure know a lot about Nigel's bike," Desreen noted.

Rodney jabbed Naddih's arm. "Okay, Mr. Know-it-all,

what about this metal rod sticking out of the back frame?"

"It's to carry passengers. You know, so you can make money!" Naddih roared with laughter.

"And what about this...and this...and...."

"If you guys keep asking me questions about the bike, we will never go ridin' today," said Naddih.

"But wait," said Desreen. "Why are there holes in the handlebars?"

Rodney piped in quickly before Naddih could answer. "To carry *nunchuckles*."

"Nunchucks? Rodney, that makes no sense," murmured Sterlin.

"And see this hook?" Naddih added. "It's to carry Nigel's handkerchief if he is sweating too much."

Desreen was astonished. She had never seen a bike with so many contraptions.

Naddih gathered them closer and lowered his voice. He glanced over his shoulder to make sure none of the neighbors who lived close by could hear him. Hooking his thumb through his belt loop, he raised his eyebrow and smiled at Desreen. Then he slowly opened a secret compartment in the seat.

"Take a look at this," he whispered.

"Ooooo," they all said, staring in awe.

"I didn't know about that," Sterlin said as his jaw dropped. "Wow! That is cool."

"What do you think he puts in there?" wondered Desreen.

"Hot sauce," replied Rodney. "Hot sauce, for sure."

"Hot sauce?" Desreen crinkled her lip. "Why would he put hot sauce in there?"

"Because, you never know when someone is going to give you a piece of chicken or pork to eat. Plus, my father says everybody should have a bottle of hot sauce on them at all times, ha-ha!"

"Rodney, you're so silly!" Desreen giggled, and they all burst out laughing.

Naddih quietly closed the secret compartment. There was no other bike in town like it and they felt lucky that Nigel let them borrow it. Flyin' on this super bike was going to be amazing!

"Come on, let's get to the hill," Suhcrom said anxiously. "We have some flyin' to do."

CHAPTER 3

Flyin' Bike—Take Two

"So, Desreen, what is your friend's name?" asked Suhcrom as they reached the gate.

"This is Muffet. She's visiting from the country. But she's kind of shy. She doesn't talk much."

Muffet smiled timidly and looked down at the ground as she took hold of Desreen's hand.

"Which country? St. Elizabeth?" Rodney asked.

"You know that's not the only other parish we have in Jamaica," said Sterlin.

"*Mi know, mi know,*" Rodney replied. "There's Kingston, St. Elizabeth, St. Catherine, Westmoreland... we have fourteen parishes. But when I hear the name 'Muffet,' I think of St. Elizabeth. *Di names dem rhyme.*"

"Rodney, don't start with your foolishness."

"I'm not starting with anything. It's true. There are fourteen parishes."

"I know that, Rodney, but Muffet does not rhyme with St. Elizabeth," Sterlin chuckled.

"It rhymes."

"Okay, okay, Rodney. Let's just get to the hill."

Together, the group of friends passed through the massive gate and pranced across the soccer field, bike in tow. They headed towards the Hart Academy, an all-boys trade school that had been under construction for quite some time. When they reached the Hart Academy, they looked for some plywood and cinder blocks. Then they went right to work to set up their bike ramp. Naddih, Rodney, and Desreen stacked the cinder blocks while Sterlin and Suhcrom retrieved a large piece of plywood.

"Hey guys, this must be our lucky day. Look what I found." Rodney pointed to a coconut tree branch.

"Yippee!" Muffet shouted with excitement.

"I thought she didn't talk," Rodney whispered to Naddih.

"Yeh, me too," said Naddih. "Hey Rodney, use that branch to clear us a path."

"So, now you're giving me orders?"

"Rodney, make sure you sweep away any broken glass or nails...anything that could cause a flat tire," Desreen cautioned. "We can't fly on a flat tire!"

"Wait a minute. Is everybody going to boss me around today?"

"No one is bossing you around," said Suhcrom. "Give me the branch, Rodney. I will do it."

"No, man, leave my broom alone. I will do it."

While Rodney carefully swept the path leading to the ramp, Sterlin and Suhcrom finished putting the plywood in place. It was propped against six cinder blocks, one stacked on top of the other, giving the ramp the steepest incline they could get.

"Have you guys seen the movie *E. T.?*" asked Desreen. "There's a part where the boy, Elliott, and E. T. fly on a bike."

"No, I haven't seen it," said Naddih. "But it's showing at Vincenzo's Theater. I want to go see it."

Rodney paused from sweeping and rested his chin on the tip of the coconut branch. "Is E.T. a superhero?"

"No, he's an alien, but he has special powers. And when Elliott protects E.T. from the bad guys, he gets on his bike and E.T. makes them fly to the moon!" Desreen exclaimed.

"To the moon? How can anyone fly to the moon on a bike?" laughed Rodney.

"It's a movie, Rodney. Anything is possible in a movie," Sterlin chuckled.

"You know, I once saw a movie where a boy was riding on the back of a...." Desreen started to relay another story when they were all called to attention.

"Ramp's ready," shouted Suhcrom. "Let's FLY!"

"Let's FLY!" Naddih echoed.

"Yeh, let's fly HIGH, like a bird in the SKY," Rodney squealed as he twirled around in a circle, flapping his arms up and down.

"How far up the hill should we go?" asked Naddih.

"To the top!" Rodney shouted.

Sterlin shook his head. "No, man. I am not starting up that high," he cautioned. "It's too steep. Somebody could get hurt."

"Yes, somebody could get hurt. Let's start about half-way." Suhcrom gently nudged Naddih's arm and whispered, "Do you remember the last time we went to the top of this hill? The wind blew us off. I ended up hitting my head, and you landed at the bottom with a mouthful of mud!"

"I want to go first," Sterlin said as he hopped on to Nigel's bike. He began to ride back and forth and around in circles to get warmed up. "Suhcrom, help me carry this bike up the hill."

Sterlin hopped off the bike and grabbed one of the handlebars while Suhcrom took hold of the back wheel. They struggled to keep their footing as they climbed up through the sandy dirt, and it became difficult for both of them to carry the bike.

"This is far enough," Sterlin said.

Sterlin prepared for his ride while Suhcrom ran back

down the hill to join the group. Sterlin knew he could fly
this bike better than the rest of them, and he wanted to
give them a good show!

"Let's see who can stay airborne the longest,"
Suhcrom said. "Naddih, you count."

"I can't count. I'm busy planning my *stratification*."

Desreen covered her mouth to hide her laughter.
She did very well in her English class and had recently
won the Spelling Bee competition at school. She knew
Naddih hadn't used the right word. She thought of cor-
recting him, but no one else seemed to notice except
Suhcrom — and he just rolled his eyes.

"Maybe Muffet will count," suggested Rodney.

"No," said Desreen, patting Muffet on the back. "I
will count."

"*Den how she a go learn fi talk gud if Desreen always
a talk fi her?*" Naddih whispered to Rodney.

"You know I can hear everything you're saying,"
Desreen replied.

Rodney and Naddih sheepishly smiled at her and
shrugged their shoulders.

Meanwhile, up on the hill, Sterlin rocked the bike
forward and backward, warming up for his ride. He dug
his heels into the dirt, ready to show his friends what
he could do.

Suhcrom glanced at Desreen to start the count. He took off his shirt and waved it in the air. "On your mark...get set...GO!"

Sterlin let loose down the hill. When he hit the bottom, he swiftly flew up the ramp with great speed, soaring smoothly through the air. There was total silence as they watched in amazement at how high Sterlin flew, and then how softly he landed. It was a perfect ride.

"Yippee!" Muffet cheered. She jumped up and down with such excitement.

Naddih tapped Desreen's arm and chuckled. "I thought you said she doesn't talk much."

"Let's see what you guys have to show now," shouted Sterlin. "Let's see who can go the highest, and who can be the most daring!"

So the competition began—first Suhcrom, then Desreen, and then Naddih. Suhcrom rode equally as well as Sterlin. But when Desreen got on the bike, everyone held their breath in awe. Not only was her ride faster, she did a wheelie in the air before landing. They all cheered her accomplishment.

Next was Naddih. He needed help from both Suhcrom and Sterlin to get the bike up the hill. Out of breath, he gave his pants a quick tug and hopped onto the seat. He knew he couldn't outshine Desreen's wheelie, but there was a chance he could stay airborne a few seconds longer. He was going for it! He took in a deep breath and away he went. He sailed down the hill and flew up the ramp, his cape flapping in the breeze. "Look at me, I'M FLYING!" he shouted. There was nothing like the freedom of soaring through the air—supercharged by the sun beating on his face, while the wind carried him high, high, high into the sky! He could hear the applause from below as he glided through the air, landing safely on the ground like an airplane on the runway.

Finally, after waiting anxiously, it was Rodney's turn.

"Guys, help me take the bike to the top of the hill."

"What? Are you crazy, man?" Suhcrom shrieked.

"Yes, I'm going to fly from the top of the hill!"

"No, Rodney, no. That's dangerous," said Desreen. "It's not safe."

"Desreen is right. Don't do it," Sterlin ordered.

"That's not fair. You guys had your turns and did what you wanted. Now it's my turn. I want to go to the top," Rodney said, sniffling. His eyes filled with tears. "And no one is going to stop me."

"Okay, Rodney, stop your bawling. I'll help you. But don't say we didn't warn you."

Suhcrom forged up to the peak of the hill, both

Rodney and the bike in tow. He paused to look at the view. It was beautiful, just as he remembered from his nomad adventure. He could see for miles. The wind began to pick up, tossing the dirt about in cylindrical clouds around them, pricking their eyes.

Rodney rubbed his hand across his face. "I sure could use some goggles."

"You can't see?"

"I can see," he said, squinting. He blinked his eyes and shouted, "I'm ready!"

"Wait, hold on until I get back down the hill," said Suhcrom.

He took a few leaps and jumps but was only halfway down the hill when he saw a look of fear across the faces of the others below. *WHOOSH!* Suddenly he felt a gush of air as Rodney blasted past him like a speeding bullet. The force knocked him over, causing him to tumble.

Rodney, flying faster than he had ever ridden before, wobbled and teetered side to side uncontrollably. He lost his grip on the handlebars, nearly missing the ramp. Then he let out the most bloodcurdling scream they had ever heard.

"*AAAAAAH!*" Rodney and the bike separated in mid-air.

"*Dis nuh luk gud fi Rodney,*" Naddih moaned.

THUD! Rodney landed face down in the dirt. *CRASH!* Nigel's bike slammed into the ground next to him, crumpling into a heap. Stunned from the impact, Rodney lay still, barely breathing.

"*Yu tink him dead?*" Naddih stared at his friend. "Maybe we should *pump him leg.*"

"No, man, don't touch him. He can't be dead. That boy has nine lives," said Suhcrom.

Naddih waved his hand at Desreen. "Go and get your mother. Isn't she a nurse?"

"No, man, no," cautioned Sterlin. "She will tell our father."

"*Waata, waata, somebody get some waata,*" Suhcrom shouted.

"*Wi out inna di field, man. Weh wi a go find waata out yah?*" asked Naddih.

"The boy doesn't need water," said Sterlin. "Shh... watch this." He leaned down next to Rodney and whispered in his ear. "I wonder if mummy is still cooking curry chicken and rice for dinner tonight," Sterlin chuckled softly.

Suddenly Rodney moaned and rolled over on his back. His eyelids fluttered and he began to smack his lips together.

"Did somebody say curry chicken and rice?" A silly

grin spread across his face, dirt caked in between his teeth. *Cough-cough. Cough-cough.* He blinked his eyes a few more times. "Guys, did you see that?"

"Man, you almost killed yourself," said Naddih.

"He's alive!" shouted Desreen.

They all started cheering and clapping. Sterlin let out a huge bellow of air, relieved that his little brother was okay. He helped him up off the ground, got him on his feet again, and brushed the dirt from his clothes.

"I'm glad you're okay, Rodney. But we won't be doing any more bike flyin' today," Suhcrom moaned. He picked up the crumpled bike. The handlebars were bent, the fender was twisted, a spoke was broken, and the front tire was flat. "When Nigel sees his bike, he's going to be mad."

CHAPTER 4

What Can a Dollar Buy?

Sterlin and Naddih each wrapped an arm around Rodney, carrying him in between them as they hobbled along. Desreen and Muffet led the way across the soccer field back to Palmerston Close. Even though most of them had great rides, their spirits were a little deflated over Rodney's near-death experience. On top of that, Nigel's bike was ruined. How were they going to explain this?

"Who is going to break the news to Nigel?" Naddih asked.

"Yeh, who's going to tell Nigel that his bike got destroyed?" asked Rodney. His lazy eye twirled around in his head as he stumbled over the rough pebbles in the dirt.

"You," said Suhcrom. "You're the one who broke it."

"But...but we all took a ride on it." Rodney's lip quivered, and then he began to whimper. He looked up at Sterlin and Suhcrom with sad eyes. As a tear ran down his cheek, he stuck out his tongue to lick the salty water at the corner of his lips.

"Rodney's right," said Desreen. "We all rode it. Let's go together to tell him."

They all agreed and Rodney sighed with relief. His head hung low as he clutched his arms around Sterlin's and Naddih's waists. The thought of telling Nigel about the bike made him dizzy. Suddenly, he spotted something tangled in a patch of weeds...something peculiar. The sunlight shone directly on it, making it stand out among the gangly grass.

"What is that?" he exclaimed excitedly.

Rodney let go of Sterlin and Naddih and darted towards the object, pointing as he ran. Everyone gasped in disbelief. It seemed he had miraculously regained his strength. The object Rodney spotted was so small that the others couldn't even see it. He picked up the crumpled ball of paper, unfolded it, and waived it in front of them.

"Look, guys, look. I found a dollar bill," he shouted. "A whole dollar. We're rich! Let's use this to fix Nigel's bike."

The group of friends looked in awe at each other. A dollar bill! They started jumping up and down, cheering and clapping their hands.

"Man, what is up with you? How do you do that?" Suhcrom said, shaking his head. "You're always finding money, Rodney."

"Yippee!" Muffet squealed.

"Is that all she ever says?" Naddih whispered to Desreen. He glanced at Muffet, raised his eyebrow and smiled. He thought she was cute, but he was curious about her shyness.

"Rodney, a dollar isn't going to be enough to fix this broken bike. But it will help," said Sterlin. "We'll go see Mr. Burke when we get home...after we tell Nigel."

The late morning sun beat down upon their heads as they rambled awkwardly through the streets to Palmerston Close. Soon they arrived at Nigel's house. They laid the crumple bike at his gate. *Clunk!*

"So...we're all going to tell him, right?" asked Rodney. They all nodded in agreement. "Suhcrom, you can start first, and then Naddih...and then Sterlin... and, and then Desreen...and then I'll jump in."

"Sure, Rodney, whatever you say."

Nigel's mom heard the commotion and came to the door. She looked squarely into the eyes of six disheartened children.

"Oh my," she exclaimed. "What is going on out here?"

"Hi, Miss Nigel's mom," they all chimed together. "Can we speak to Nigel please?"

She cast a questioning look over the entire group. "Nigel," she called out. "It's Suhcrom and Naddih, and their friends. *Nigel, yu hear mi a call yu name?* Come here. They want to talk to you."

When Nigel appeared at the door, he saw the look on their faces. He glanced past them to where the bike lay on the ground and instantly saw the twisted handlebars. Usually, he was rather meek-mannered and didn't get upset at much of anything. But this was his bike, his only bike — his super bike. He felt the anger building up inside. His throat tightened as disappointment spread across his face.

"Is that MY bike?"

"Yes," Naddih paused. "It's your bike."

"What did you do to it?"

"I didn't do anything to it. Ask Rodney," replied Naddih. He jabbed Rodney's arm. "Rodney, tell him. Tell him what you did."

"That's not the order we agreed on," Rodney began to whimper. "Suhcrom, you go first, then you, Naddih, then Sterlin, then Desreen, and then me."

"I'll tell him," said Suhcrom. He stepped to the front of the group and stood face to face with Nigel. "We're sorry, Nigel. We all took turns riding. We were having a great time, and then Rodney wanted to be a big man and show off. He went up the hill a little too far, and when he came down and hit the ramp, well...he flew up in the air, right off the bike. He slammed into the ground, and the bike came crashing down."

"We all thought he was dead," Desreen sighed.

"I'm really sorry, Nigel. But look, I found a dollar...a whole dollar! Do you want it?" Rodney asked enthusiastically.

"No, I don't want your dollar. I want my bike back—the same way I gave it to you."

"We are going to see Mr. Burke right now to get it fixed," added Sterlin.

The lines of anger in Nigel's face began to disappear and his voice softened at hearing Mr. Burke's name. "Mr. Burke can fix it. I know he can. He's worked on it before. But tell him I need it in a week. I'm in the big race next Saturday, remember?"

"Oh yes, the big race," exclaimed Naddih. "People from all over are going to be here."

"Don't worry, Nigel," said Rodney. "We'll make sure your bike is the best bike in the race!"

"So how am I going to train with no bike?"

"You can use mine," said Desreen.

"And we can help you train," Naddih offered. "We will do it as a team."

"Do you know how to train people?" asked Suhcrom.

"I don't know about your trainings, Naddih," said

Nigel. "The last time we trained together, we were out in the rain, running through mud and crawling under wire like we were in boot camp learning to be soldiers. And that was just for one soccer match against the Waterford boys!"

"But we won, didn't we?" Naddih chuckled.

Nigel looked at Desreen and gave her offer some thought. "I've seen your bike. It's pretty cool.... Okay," he agreed.

"We can start training tomorrow morning," Desreen stated. "You don't have a lot of time."

With the issue of training settled, Suhcrom picked up Nigel's twisted bike and the group headed over to Mr. Burke's place. They found him in his backyard wiping grease off the muffler of his old beat-up '57 Chevy. He swung his head around just as the boys hollered out his name.

"Hi, Mr. Burke," Sterlin called out.

Suhcrom and Naddih waved to him and smiled.

"Well, hello boys. What can I do for you?" said Mr. Burke. He tucked his greasy rag in his back pocket and sat down on a nearby bench.

Suhcrom didn't waste any time getting right to the point. "We need to get Nigel's bike fixed. He has a race next Saturday. Can you do it?"

"We have a whole dollar to pay for it," Rodney added.

Mr. Burke looked at the bike for several minutes. "Hmm...let me see." He scratched his head and mumbled some words that none of the kids could understand. Then he jotted down some numbers on a pad of paper.

"*A weh him a seh?*" Rodney asked.

"Don't worry about it, man. He's talking grown-up talk. Us kids usually can't understand them," replied Naddih.

"Yeh, this is why we get into trouble and they have to tell us things over and over."

"Well, kids, you don't have much of a bike left. It's going to need new handlebars, a new tire, new spokes, and a new fender. I will have to check to see what parts I have here, but it is going to cost more than a dollar to fix it."

"So how much will it be?" asked Naddih.

"It's going to cost about eight dollars."

Gulp! Their jaws dropped.

"Did he say eight dollars?" Rodney whispered.

"Yes, Rodney, you're standing right in front of him. Open up your ears," said Naddih.

"Tell you what," Mr. Burke continued, "I'll do it for four dollars and seventy five cents."

"Yippee!" Muffet shouted.

"Here's the one dollar. Will this get things started?" Rodney asked as he pulled the dollar bill from his pocket.

"You can hold on to it for now, Rodney, and pay me later."

"NO! No way," they all shouted. "If he holds onto it we will never see it again."

"He will buy junk food and stuff his little belly," Suhcrom laughed.

"Okay," agreed Mr. Burke. "I will hold onto it."

Rodney placed the money in Mr. Burke's hand. "Nigel needs his bike fixed really bad. We want him to win."

"I want him to win, too." Mr. Burke smiled.

"Can you make it the best bike in the race?" Rodney asked.

"I'll see what I can do."

"Thank you, Mr. Burke," said Rodney.

"Yes, thanks, Mr. Burke," said Naddih.

Suhcrom shook Mr. Burke's hand. "We will pick up the bike on Friday."

"Okay, run along now kids. I have a lot of work to do if this bike is going to be ready on time," Mr. Burke replied, waving them out of his yard.

As they left Mr. Burke's place, Naddih's brain swirled around with hundreds of ideas on how they could raise money to pay for Nigel's bike. His eyes grew wide, and he had a grin that spread from ear to ear.

"I have an idea," he shouted. "We could make chicken back and dumplin' and sell it to all the neighbors!"

"I can bake cookies," Desreen said eagerly. "Everybody likes my cookies. Muffet, you can help me."

"I don't know, Naddih," Rodney said hesitantly. "The last time we made dumplin' together it didn't turn out so good. Not good at all."

"Ha-ha, I thought you liked them, Rodney. You ate five big dumplings and then laid on the ground complaining about how you couldn't move!" Suhcrom laughed as he recalled his first attempt at cooking....

...It all began last year, one early summer morning, when Rodney came knocking on Suhcrom and Naddih's bedroom window. The rattling of the thin glass pane startled both of them.

"What are you doing here?" asked Naddih, rubbing his eyes. "Are you here for business or for pleasure?"

"What?"

"Business or pleasure."

"I don't know what you're talking about."

"Never mind, Rodney. You need to watch more television," Naddih chuckled. "Why are you here so early?"

"Suhcrom said we're going fishing in the gully this morning."

"We are," Suhcrom mumbled. He hopped out of bed and tossed a shirt over his head. "Naddih, grab those jelly jars we cleaned out yesterday, and let's get out of here before Enomih starts bossing us around and makes us take out the garbage."

They scurried out of the house in their bare feet, and with Rodney trailing slightly behind, the three boys headed across the street towards the gully. They hadn't gone far when Rodney suddenly screamed out.

"Ha-ha! Guys, look...look...I found a dollar!"

Suhcrom and Naddih couldn't believe their eyes. It was dirty and wrinkled, but it was indeed a one-dollar bill. They all shouted for joy.

"What should we do with it?" asked Naddih.

"Let's get some bun and cheese and bulla cake. *Mi so hungry, man.*" Rodney rubbed his belly.

"You're always hungry for junk food. I think we should cook something," Naddih suggested.

"Who is going to cook?" asked Rodney.

"Not Enomih," Suhcrom murmured. "If she finds out

we have a dollar she will take it from us. This has to be our secret."

Rodney and Naddih stared at Suhcrom. Naddih tipped his head and smirked.

"You can cook. Me and Rodney are too young. You are the oldest, so you should do it."

"Yeh, Suhcrom, you cook, because Naddih adds ketchup and black pepper to everything, even chocolate cake."

"*Unu no know notin 'bout flava,*" Naddih mumbled.

After some hesitation, Suhcrom finally agreed. He took charge of the dollar and tucked it safely in his pocket. The fishing adventure was cancelled and they set off to see the Shopkeeper Lady. On their way to the store, the boys talked about what to cook.

"Let's make jerk chicken or pork," suggested Naddih.

Rodney licked his lips and rubbed his belly. "That sounds yummy!"

Suhcrom curled his lip and shook his head. "Man, I don't know how to cook jerk chicken or pork. Besides, I don't think a dollar is enough to buy all of that."

"So what can we get?" asked Rodney.

"We will see," replied Suhcrom. "Rodney, you wait here by the gate. If you and Naddih both go inside the store, one of you will give our secret away. Naddih, you come with me," Suhcrom whispered. "But let me do all the talking."

The Shopkeeper Lady squinted suspiciously at the boys as they entered the store.

"Howdy, Suhcrom and Naddih. Are you boys here for another cardboard box?"

Suhcrom chuckled quietly under his breath as he put the money on the counter. He brushed some of the dirt off of it and tried to flatten the wrinkles.

"No, no box today. I was wondering, what could we buy with this money in terms of food?" he asked politely. "Will it get us some chicken and flour?"

The Shopkeeper Lady kindly smiled at them. She explained that it was enough for half a pound of flour, but not enough for chicken. So she offered to add in some chicken back.

"Chicken back? There's no meat on that. That's all bones," Suhcrom moaned. "Could you at least toss in a leg?"

The Shopkeeper Lady snickered at the thought of Suhcrom and Naddih bargaining with her. She crossed her arms and shifted her feet as she pondered what to do.

"Tell you what," she said, winking at Naddih. "I'll throw in a couple chicken necks."

From the gate, Rodney's ears perked up. "Did she say chicken neck? I love chicken neck!"

"Is that Rodney? Why is he sticking his face through the metal bars?" she wondered. "Why didn't he just come in?"

"Because he talks too much," Suhcrom muttered.

Naddih watched excitedly as she wrapped the food in newspaper. With the last knot tied in the string, the boys paid for the food and hustled out of the store.

Naddih turned around and waved as they left. "Thanks, Miss Shopkeeper Lady. Buddha bless you."

"Buddha bless you? Man, that's why I don't let you talk."

Once they got outside the gate, Rodney joined them and they headed for home. Their walk turned into a slow jog. Before long, the slow jog turned into a full-speed run back to the house. Their father was still at work and Enomih had gone to a friend's house, so they were all alone. Their father had warned them never to use the kerosene stove in the house when there were no adults around. But they really wanted to cook, so they decided to use the coal stove in the backyard.

"Rodney, I am going to get the stove started," said Suhcrom. He struck the match to light the fire, and then gave Rodney some wadded up newspaper to fan it.

"Keep an eye on it and let me know when the water's boiling, okay? Just keep fanning it so the coal will burn. And remember, keep your distance from the fire."

Meanwhile, there was chaos in the kitchen. Naddih had been in charge of cutting up the vegetables. Onion peels and tomato seeds were all over the counter and streams of tomato juice splattered the walls and floor. It looked like a war zone!

"The vegetables are ready," Naddih said proudly.

Suhcrom made the curried chicken back and chicken neck, and then started the dumplings. He had watched his grandmother make them a number of times before. It looked so easy. All he needed was flour, water and salt. Not knowing how much of each ingredient was needed, he decided to pour in what he thought looked good...a little flour, a little water and a little salt—*oops!* The lid on the salt box popped off and a heaping mound of salt landed on the dough.

"Oh no," Suhcrom moaned. "That's way too much salt!"

He spooned out as much of it as he could, and just as he was about to roll out the dough, Rodney came running into the house, screaming frantically.

"My eyes! My eyes! I can't see!" Rodney rubbed his puffy red eyes. Tears streamed down his cheeks.

"What's wrong, Rodney?" asked Suhcrom. "Open your eyes, man. Open your eyes."

"I can't. The smoke...," whined Rodney. "I fanned the fire with newspaper just like you said, Suhcrom, and it was burning really good—too good. It got too high, so I blew on it to cool it down and the smoke...." Rodney rubbed his eyes again.

"You blew on it? Who told you to do that?"

"You always blow on things to cool them down."

"You're not supposed to blow on it, Rodney. Now you know why. You okay?"

"My eyes are burning."

"Let's go to the sink and wash them out," said Suhcrom. "Then we'll check to see if the water is boiling."

After the dumplings were done, and the chicken back and neck were cooked, the boys sat down to eat. It smelled delicious! Naddih and Rodney dug in eagerly— but not Suhcrom. He took one bite of the dumpling and spit it out.

"Man, I'm not eating that."

He watched Naddih and Rodney with anticipation, anxious to see what they would say. Naddih ate slowly, taking tiny little bites. He nodded his head in quiet approval, taking gulps of water between each bite. Rodney chowed down five dumplings one right after another. He coughed and gagged in between, begging Naddih for some of his water.

"*Man, di dumplin' dem salty,*" said Rodney as he flopped on the ground. "*But gud, Suhcrom. Mi belly full.*"

In spite of the compliments, Suhcrom threw out the rest of the dumplings and declared the whole thing a failure....

❧

Suhcrom chuckled again, remembering his disastrous attempt at cooking.

"No, guys. I don't think cooking is a good idea," he said. "Unless you want to sell salty dumplings!"

"Why don't we collect bottles and cans and take them to the grocery store for money," suggested Sterlin.

"That's a great idea," shouted Naddih.

"I think that is a good idea, too," agreed Desreen.

"Okay, let's meet up tomorrow in front the Hart Academy. We'll start with those houses first," said Suhcrom. "And bring your *crocus bags!*"

CHAPTER 5

Bottles and Cans

Knock-knock-knock.

"Is anybody home?" Naddih asked.

Knock-knock-knock.

"Why did you knock again, Rodney? Didn't you just see me knock?"

"I didn't hear any footsteps," Rodney said quietly. "Grown-ups always have heavy footsteps."

"Just leave the door alone."

They waited a few more seconds and still no one came to the door. Rodney knocked again a little harder. This time he did it so hard, it made the door rattle.

They heard a woman's voice call out loudly. *"A weh unu a beat down mi door fa? Unu a police?"*

Naddih and Rodney giggled into their hands.

"She thinks we're the police," said Rodney.

"Who is it?" she asked through the closed door.

"It's me, Rodney and Muffet."

"Who is 'me'?" she asked as she opened the door.

When their eyes met hers, she smiled. She was a

stout woman wearing a bright-colored skirt with a tee shirt that said "Irie Mornin', Jamaica."

She examined the three youngsters who were standing in front of her in silence, staring up at her. Rodney nudged Naddih. Then Naddih nudged Rodney while Muffet looked off in the other direction.

"Kids, how can I help you?"

Rodney leaned over and whispered to Naddih, "You talk."

"Hold on, Miss. I have this piece of paper in my pocket. I wrote something on it to tell you."

Naddih fumbled around in his pocket and pulled out a wadded piece of paper. He cleared his throat, took a deep breath, and then cleared his throat again.

"Man, just talk. The lady is waiting."

Naddih gave Rodney a dirty look. "You want to talk then?"

"No, you go ahead."

"My name is Naddih."

"I've seen you before. You're one of the kids who carried that big cardboard box back and forth in front of my house."

"Oh, okay. So I guess you know who I am," Naddih said. "Well, this is Rodney, and this is Muffet. She doesn't talk much."

"It's nice to meet all of you. My name is Miss Paulette. I see you have a crocus bag, Naddih. What are you here for?"

Naddih looked at the script he had carefully prepared the night before. He began reading. "We are collecting bottles and cans to fix Nigel's bike because Rodney broke it."

Rodney glared at Naddih and gave his arm a quick jab.

"Nigel's bike needs to be fixed for the race, Miss Paulette," he added. "Any bottles you can give us will help a lot."

Miss Paulette peered at Muffet and spoke softly as she smiled. "Do you have anything you want to say?"

Muffet shook her head. She twirled her finger through her hair and shifted her eyes downward.

"She's shy. She's visiting from the country," Rodney explained.

"Oh, I see." Miss Paulette grinned. "Well, kids, I don't know who Nigel is, but he's very lucky to have friends like you who want to help him. You wait here. Let me see what bottles I may have."

When she returned, she brought with her a big crate of glass soda bottles. Their eyes lit up with excitement as they filled each of their crocus bags.

"Yippee," Muffet grinned. She shrugged her shoulders and giggled softly when Miss Paulette looked at her and smiled.

"That's all she ever says, Miss Paulette," Rodney chuckled.

"Thanks for the bottles, ma'am," said Naddih.

The trio dragged their nearly full bags out of the yard and moved on. Just as they entered the gate of the next neighbor's yard, they caught sight of Suhcrom a couple houses over.

"Look at all the bottles we have!" Naddih shouted. He waved and signaled a "two thumbs up" to his brother.

Meanwhile, Suhcrom, Sterlin and Desreen were not having as much luck. The neighbor they were talking to was a little grouchy, insisting that he needed his bottles and cans for himself. However, he offered to pay Suhcrom ten cents towards his worthy cause.

"Ten cents? That's two bottles worth. Can't you just give me the two bottles?" asked Suhcrom.

"Okay then," the man muttered. "Here are two bottles to help fix your friend's bike."

Dragging their bags, the kids continued to go from house to house, collecting a few bottles here and a few cans there. Eventually, they hit all the houses in the surrounding neighborhood, stretching from the Hart

Academy to all of Palmerston Close. They had worked hard, and it was time to go to the store and cash in what they collected.

The Shopkeeper Lady beamed from ear to ear when she saw Suhcrom and Naddih again. She cast a curious look at the lumpy crocus bags and raised her eyebrow.

"What do you have there?"

"We have lots of bottles and cans," said Desreen excitedly.

"Hmm, bottles and cans, huh?"

"This bag is so heavy, it must be worth five thousand dollars!" said Naddih.

The Shopkeeper Lady snickered. "Well, at five cents per bottle, Naddih, I don't think it will be worth that much."

"Holy Moly! A whole five cents for every bottle?" Rodney jumped in the air and pumped his fist. *Pow!* "Can we use some of the money to buy icy mint candy?"

"NO RODNEY," they all shouted in unison.

"The money is to fix Nigel's bike," said Sterlin.

The Shopkeeper Lady began to sort the bottles and cans and asked them to bring her a few of the discarded boxes from outside the store. When the kids returned, they helped her empty out the crocus bags. Bottles went into one box and cans into the other. They worked fast and furiously, and chatted while sorting.

"Is it true, Desreen?" asked Rodney as he started to toss a bottle to Naddih. *Crash!* The bottle slipped from Rodney's hand and shattered on the concrete floor. Naddih narrowed his eyes and scowled.

"Ooops...take dat outta mi ration," Rodney sighed.

"Is what true, Rodney?" asked Desreen.

Rodney's gaze darted back and forth between Desreen and Naddih. "Why are you looking at me that way, Naddih? I didn't spill the secret."

"What secret?" they all asked at the same time. Everyone, including the Shopkeeper Lady, stopped what they were doing. Their heads turned and their ears perked up. All eyes were on Rodney.

"Well...." He paused for a moment. "I heard that Delroy, the bad boy from the Box Juice Gang, was picking on Darius at school one day during recess, and that all the boys and girls on the soccer field gathered around them, shouting, 'Fight, fight. There's gonna be a fight!' Then you jumped in the middle, shoved Delroy, then put him in a headlock and punched him twice, knocking him to the ground. Then you sat on him and told him to apologize."

"Mi neva tell yu dat," Naddih muttered.

Desreen laughed. "Yes, some of that is true. I did push Delroy. I pushed him away and told him to leave Darius alone. But that was all."

"Are you sure you didn't punch him?" asked Rodney.

"Didn't you hear what she said? She didn't punch him," replied Sterlin.

"You watch too much boxing," laughed Suhcrom.

"Punching someone is wrong," said Desreen.

"That was brave of you," said Naddih.

"Yeh, Delroy and his Box Juice Gang are known for picking on kids at school. Everyone is afraid of them," said Sterlin.

"We should always stand up for people who can't defend themselves. That was the right thing to do, Desreen," said the Shopkeeper Lady.

"Can I tell you about the time I stood up for Roscoe?" Naddih asked.

"No, Naddih. We don't have time," Suhcrom sighed. "We have to finish counting the bottles."

"I think you already told me that story," Rodney mumbled. "Do I have to listen to it again?"

"I think I've heard it, too," said Sterlin.

"Wait, how come Rodney can tell his story and I can't tell mine?"

"But that was Desreen's story, not mine," laughed Rodney.

"*Dats not di point.*" Naddih frowned. "Everybody gets to do what they want to do but me. Like you,

Rodney, you got to take the bike to the top of the hill even though everybody said it was a bad idea, and look what happened. You...."

"Okay, okay, Naddih. Tell your story," Desreen chuckled.

"It all started one hot, windy Monday afternoon when...."

"Tell us the short version," Suhcrom interrupted.

"Well, Roscoe asked me if we were still going to play soccer with the boys from fifth grade. I told him those boys play rough and they are much bigger than us. But he said we could learn a lot from them. So after we ate some stew peas and rice and carrot juice at the canteen, we went out to the field."

Suhcrom jabbed Naddih's arm. "The short version, man."

"Yes, yes, just be patient, man. I had just made this great save when Roscoe joined the game. He had taken off his shirt, shoes and socks because he didn't want to get them dirty."

"So what happened?" asked Desreen.

"We lined up at center field, and a new game started. Roscoe was right there in the middle of the action, dancing and making all kinds of fancy moves, dribbling the ball down the field. When he got to the six-yard box, he kicked the ball with all of his might. *Rrrrrrrrrrip!* His pants split open—I mean, WIDE open...everything was showing. All the boys swarmed around Roscoe, laughing and tugging at his pants, shouting, 'Roscoe's ripped! Roscoe's ripped!'"

"He must have been so embarrassed," sighed Rodney.

"And then, he started to cry. I felt really bad for him. I didn't like the way they were making fun of him, either. So I jumped in the middle and pulled him away. I took my shirt off so he could cover up his pants, and we walked off the field together."

"That was very kind of you to help your friend when the other boys were being so cruel," said the Shopkeeper Lady.

"I bet Roscoe was happy you gave him your shirt," said Suhcrom.

"Yes, Naddih," Desreen agreed. "And it was a brave act to jump in the middle and pull Roscoe away from those boys."

"Okay, children, it's getting late. Let's do another brave act and clean up this broken glass before someone gets hurt," said the Shopkeeper Lady. "Here are a couple of brooms. You kids clean up while I cash in your bottles and cans."

She rang up the register and handed two dollars and seventy-five cents to Sterlin.

"Oh man, we're still a dollar short?" Naddih shook his head. "That's not enough."

"We can't go back to Mr. Burke's place until we have all the money," said Sterlin.

"Hey guys, you know what? Let's go to the swamp," suggested Suhcrom. "People leave bottles and cans there all the time. Maybe we can find some bike parts there, too."

Suhcrom and Sterlin led the way. Naddih, Rodney, Desreen and Muffet followed at a distance, but they still had Suhcrom and Sterlin in their sights as they went down the road.

The area beyond the road sloped slightly downhill toward the swamp. The grass was damp and the almond trees rustled in the gentle sea breeze. Just past the almond trees, the bamboo reeds grew plentiful, and the mud became darker and thicker.

Because of the slope of the land, Suhcrom and Sterlin didn't see the wild dogs feasting on discarded food. Had they known, they would have turned and run. But they weren't paying attention. Suddenly, Suhcrom heard a sound. It made his neck prickle. His palms got sweaty and he felt like he would have an asthma attack. He quickly felt his pocket. *Oh good, my inhaler is here.* He reached out and touched Sterlin's shoulder.

"Stop. Don't move."

Sterlin stopped immediately. "What is it?" he said in a low whisper.

"Why are you guys stopping?" Naddih hollered.

Grrrrrrr. Grrrrrr. The dogs looked up from their feast and growled at the boys.

"Holy Moly, Sterlin!"

"Don't run, Suhcrom," Sterlin said quietly.

"But look at their teeth! Run, Sterlin, run," Suhcrom shouted, scrambling up the slope. "Run, Naddih. Rodney, Desreen, Muffet—RUN!"

The pack of wild dogs charged up the hill, barking and chasing them aggressively. They all screamed. Suhcrom was filled with fear as he stumbled over his own feet, hurrying as fast as he could. The dogs chased the children down the street and past some of the houses.

Suhcrom felt the dog's hot breath behind him, its sharp teeth piercing the back of his pants. *Rrrip!* The pocket tore away from his pants while he kept running, determined not to stop until he reached the safety of his home.

The screaming children and barking dogs caused chaos as they charged into their neighborhood. One of the grown-ups grabbed a stick and waved it at the dogs.

"Shoo, shoo. Get out of here, you dogs," he shouted as they scooted away.

Out of breath, the group of friends checked with each other to make sure they were all okay.

"One of the dogs tore your pocket, Suhcrom," said Rodney.

"You run like a Jamaican *lympian*," laughed Naddih.

"You mean Olympian," corrected Sterlin.

"But he wasn't limping," said Rodney. *"Him run gud and fast pon him foot dem."*

"Rodneyyyy!" Sterlin huffed.

"I know, I know. I'm embarrassing you again. I don't say anything when you embarrass me."

"Well, Rodney, it's Olympian. *Like di people dem who go a foreign and run for Jamaica.* We have a lot of famous Olympians."

"Maybe we could ask one of those Olympians to run to the swamp for the bottles and cans because I'm never going back there again—not as long as those dogs are living there!" Suhcrom shuddered.

"How are we going to get the rest of the money we need for Nigel's bike?" asked Desreen.

"Maybe, instead of money, we could find some spare parts—like a tire or even a handlebar," suggested Naddih. "Suhcrom, let's go to Newlands to the car dump.

Mr. C-Ton always has a lot of stuff there."

"Great idea, Naddih," said Suhcrom. "Okay guys, we will meet up with you later this evening, after we get back from Newlands. Then we can help Nigel train for his race."

CHAPTER 6

Junk Yard Disaster

When Suhcrom and Naddih got to Mama's house in Newlands, everyone was happy to see them. All of their cousins, aunts and uncles who lived at the house with their grandmother were working on their daily chores. Cousin Peeko and Uncle Buckett, both of whom were younger than Suhcrom and Naddih, were out in the yard filling up tires with water.

"Hey Naddih, do you and Suhcrom want to go with us to race tires down the lane?" Peeko asked.

"Yes, let's go Suhcrom!" shouted Naddih. "Where's my tire, Peeko?"

"I hid it behind the chicken coop like you asked me to."

"Why are you hiding a silly tire? It's just a piece of junk." Suhcrom rolled his eyes.

"I didn't want anybody to steal it."

"And your silly tire is behind the chicken coop, too, Suhcrom," Buckett snickered.

"I don't want to race tires today...and maybe never again." Suhcrom shook his head.

He recalled the accident he had the last time he raced tires. He had been over at Marlon Plant chopping down trees to help Mr. Dridge make coal. To make his chores more fun, he had been pretending to be an explorer searching for wildlife when he found this really cool tire. Over the span of a month, he had raced with this special tire, never realizing how badly worn out it was. Then one day, while racing in the lane with his cousins, the friction from the sticks rubbing against the inside of the tire wore a hole right through it. When the sticks punctured the tire, they jammed against some stones and he flipped head first over the tire. He had cuts and bruises everywhere! He hurt for days afterwards, and promised never to race tires again.

"Can we at least watch the race for two minutes, Suhcrom? Please?"

"No, Naddih. We don't have time. We need to get to the junk yard and then back to Palmerston Close."

The junk yard, or "car dump" as Naddih called it, was owned by Mr. C-Ton, a former next door neighbor of Mama's. He was still a good friend of their grandfather, Mr. Stepson, and became friends with Suhcrom and Naddih because they visited so often. In fact, Mr. C-Ton invited them to come to the junk yard anytime they wanted and gave them permission to take whatever they needed.

Mr. C-Ton was a bona fide mechanic in his own right and accumulated useless cars that no longer worked. He was known to collect just about anything—from cars without engines, to cars without steering wheels, to cars with absolutely no wheels at all. He even had cars with no floors! Most of the cars in the junk yard were propped up on cinder blocks, and it wasn't unusual to see all kinds of rodents taking up residence in, and under, the cars.

Mr. C-Ton was not only a mechanic, he was also a man of many trades. He did plumbing and painting. He built fences, made bricks, and fixed just about anything around the house that people needed. But he was best known for being a butcher. He owned every single kind of knife one could imagine, and if you needed a pig, cow or goat butchered, Mr. C-Ton was the man to call. People never really talked about his mechanic skills, but when it came to butchering, he was the master—the best of the best.

When Suhcrom and Naddih reached the junk yard, Mr. C-Ton wasn't home and the gate was locked.

"Looks like we have to go over the fence," said Suhcrom.

"Not another fence!" Naddih said in despair. "Why us Jamaicans always building fences?"

"Do you think there are any dogs in there?" Suhcrom asked timidly. "I heard that Mr. C-Ton uses vicious dogs now to guard his property."

"That's not true. *Dats jus people a labba labba dem mouth, man,*" Naddih replied. He peaked through a tiny whole in the fence. "I don't see any sign that says, 'Beware of bad dogs.'"

Suhcrom raised his eyebrow. "Why would it say 'bad' dogs? Why wouldn't it just say 'Beware of dogs?'"

"That's how us Jamaicans talk. We put 'bad' in front of everything...bad dog, bad man, bad *pickney*, talk bad...."

"What? What are you talking about, man?" Suhcrom laughed. "Let's just get over the fence and look for some handlebars, and then get back home for Nigel's training."

The boys dropped to the ground inside the fence, kicking up a cloud of dust around their ankles as they landed. They were surrounded by stacks of rusty metal, piles of tires and rows of old cars.

"Holy Smackaroni, Suhcrom. This place is a gold mine! Hey Suhcrom, Suhcrom...hey Suhcrom, look."

"Man, I heard you. You don't have to keep calling out my name."

"Suhcrom, look at me." Naddih picked up an interesting pair of sunglasses and tried them on. He giggled, attempting a British accent. "Hey mate, do I look braggadocious?"

"I don't think British people use that word. Only us Jamaicans! So, Mr. British Man, what are you going to do with those sunglasses?" Suhcrom laughed.

"Wear them."

"But they only have one lens. You look silly."

"Oh wow, Suhcrom." Naddih ran over to a pile of tires. "Look at these tires...and steering wheels and reflectors...lots of reflectors." Suddenly, he spotted a particularly shiny one. He picked it out of the pile and slipped it into his pocket. "Mr. C-Ton is a real junk man. I never saw anybody collect more stuff than him, except maybe Mr. Burke...but he only has one junk car! Hey look, a broken stick."

"What are you going to do with a broken broom stick?"

"Well...I could break it in two, get a piece of string and some tape, and make *nunchuckles*," Naddih smirked. "Or just give it to Mama for firewood."

"That won't make much of a fire!" Suhcrom laughed.

"Hey Suhcrom, Suhcrom. What is this?" Naddih skipped over to a pile of old, rusty dented hubcaps. In the midst was a hubcap so shiny and new it was hard to miss.

"Suhcrom, look at this. It sticks out like a cow in a pig pen."

"Where did you hear that from?"

"From one of the grown-ups."

"Who?"

"I don't remember her name, but what I think she meant was you can't miss it. Look, it's a brand new hubcap."

"Come on, Naddih, leave that alone. We just need to find handlebars."

"But Suhcrom, it's perfect for a shield—just like they use in battle!"

"Naddih, you're giving me a headache. What do you want, a shield or parts for Nigel's bike?"

"Here, catch it, Suhcrom," Naddih yelled, tossing the hubcap like a Frisbee. "Catch it."

For a few moments, the boys forgot all about Nigel's broken bike and the rapidly approaching race. It seemed as though time stood still as they tossed the hubcap back and forth, thinking up different ways to make a game out of it.

"Throw it like a *boombalang*," said Naddih.

Suhcrom burst out laughing. "It's boomerang, and I'm not sure it will work like a boomerang."

"Throw it, Suhcrom, throw it like a *boombalang*!" shouted Naddih.

"Okay, let's see if it comes back."

Suhcrom picked up the hubcap and twirled himself around and around in a circle, gaining momentum, and then hurled the hubcap as far as he could. They watched it spin through the air. And then, suddenly, it turned.

"Aaaaaah!" Suhcrom screamed. "It's coming back—and it's coming straight at us! Watch out, Naddih, watch out."

Suhcrom grabbed Naddih's arm and pulled him to the ground. The boys hit the dirt just as the hubcap whizzed over their heads and slammed into one of the junk cars. *BANG!*

Bark! Bark-Bark! Bark-bark-bark!

Suhcrom gasped. It was the sound he dreaded most — the piercing bark of a vicious dog! He lifted his face out of the dirt and caught a glimpse of a huge shadow passing between the cars.

"Holy Moly, Naddih, run. We have to get out of here fast," he yelled. "RUN!"

Their feet barely touched the ground. Suhcrom reached the fence first and climbed to the top at record speed. Meanwhile, Naddih was still inside the junk yard, running in circles, flailing his arms and screaming wildly. The one-lens pair of sunglasses slipped crookedly across his nose.

"Hey, Naddih," Suhcrom laughed. "Stop and look behind you."

Naddih stopped as soon as he saw the dog and burst into full-bellied laughter. Never had he seen anything so funny in all of his life. He and Suhcrom had been fleeing from a dog whose hind legs were strapped to wheels and who wore a patch over its left eye. It was anything but vicious!

"Come on, man, let's just get out of here," said Suhcrom as he helped Naddih over the fence. "What were you doing back there anyway? Why were you running in circles?"

"I learned that when you are being chased by alligators, the best way to escape is to run in zigzags."

"But, Naddih, that was no alligator. That was a dog—a silly dog on wheels!"

"I saw it in a *doctamentry.*"

Suhcrom chuckled. "You're always saying *fool-fool* things, and you still haven't learned how to say 'documentary.'"

"But when you're in danger, Suhcrom, your *atrampolin* kicks in, and you will do anything to stay alive."

"I don't know about that, and I'm pretty sure *atrampolin* isn't a word."

"What about the handlebars for Nigel's bike?"

"I'm done looking for bike parts. I almost got my head chopped off playing with that hubcap and I don't want to be chased by any more dogs. Come on, we need to get back to Palmerston Close."

"Yes, we need to help Nigel train for his race on Saturday," said Naddih. "We don't have much time."

CHAPTER 7

Mr. Wheeler's Donkey Cart

As Suhcrom and Naddih passed the lane that led to their grandmother's house, they waved good-bye, but no one saw them. They had been walking for some time and the heat of the afternoon sun had melted the tar on the road, scorching the bottom of their feet.

"Holy Macaroni, Suhcrom, it's really hot out here," said Naddih. He sat down at the side of the road to rest. *"Mi tink it out fi kill wi today. Why him jus a falla wi so?"*

"Who is following us?"

"The sun, man. Everywhere we go, he is right over our heads! Why can't he just give us a break for two seconds."

"Naddih, the sun is way, way up in the sky, over everyone's head," laughed Suhcrom. "So, if that's the case, I think it's trying to kill everybody! I sure could go for a huge glass of lemonade with BIG ice cubes in it." Suhcrom licked his dry, chapped lips. "Man, I am so thirsty!"

"I could go for a huge glass of lemonade with some freezer ice in it."

"Freezer ice?"

"Yeh, the soft, slushy ice that forms on the side of the freezer."

"Yes, I like that ice, too. But sometimes it tastes really bad—like when the raw chicken or fish juice spills on it. Yuck!"

Just then the boys heard a familiar sound. *Clippety-cloppety, clippety-cloppety.* They recognized the sound of hooves pounding on the pavement. *Ah, it's Mr. Wheeler!*

Suhcrom and Naddih couldn't have been happier to hear that sound. They smiled and waved as Mr. Wheeler approached. The donkey cart was filled with coconuts, watermelons, mangos, green bananas, ripe bananas, and all different kinds of other fruits.

"I bet Mr. Wheeler is on his way to the market. He'll be passing right by Palmerston Close. Maybe we can hitch a ride on the back of his cart," said Suhcrom.

"Whoa, Jawbreaker, whoa," Mr. Wheeler hollered to the donkey. "Whoa, girl." He stopped the cart, recognizing the boys. "What are you boys doing all the way out here?"

"We went to Newlands to visit Mama," Suhcrom called out. "And now we're going back home."

"Hop on. I'll give you a ride."

"Mr. Wheeler, can I sit up front and help you steer the donkey cart?" asked Naddih.

"Sure, Naddih, grab yourself a banana and come on up."

While Naddih hopped up onto the seat next to Mr. Wheeler, Suhcrom cautiously climbed onto one of the logs that hung off the back. This was one of the biggest donkey carts he had ever seen, but he knew if he wasn't careful, the least bit of added weight could set the cart off balance, tipping the front end straight up in the air. Mr. Wheeler had lost his load of fruits more than once this way!

"Hey Suhcrom...Suhcrom, Suhcrom. Look, I'm controlling the donkey—just like those fancy people in their long red coats and their white gloves and black hats do it in the British movies. I'm not as fancy as them, though. Suhcrom, Suhcrom, are you listening to me?"

"Yes, yes, I heard you the first time Mr. Fancy British Man," Suhcrom mumbled. He stepped over a mound of coconuts and sat down against a huge pile of green bananas. *Mmm*...the sweet aroma of the fresh fruits surrounding him made him feel hungry. He grabbed a ripe banana and began to eat it as the cart jostled rhythmically along.

"Hey, Suhcrom, there's Mr. Boardy's mansion," Naddih called out. "Look, Suhcrom. Suhcrom...?"

"I think your brother has fallen asleep," said Mr. Wheeler.

"Yes, Mr. Wheeler, and probably he is counting baby goats by now," laughed Naddih.

"Sheep."

"What?"

"People count sheep when they are sleeping, not goats," he chuckled.

"It nuh mek nuh difference, Mista Wheeler. Dem both chew on grass."

Naddih wiggled backwards in the seat and tightened his hold on the reins. They didn't have much farther to go before they would reach Palmerston Close, so he wanted to slow the donkey down a bit.

Beep-beep-beep! The piercing blast of a car horn jolted Suhcrom.

"Wake up, Naddih. We're almost home."

"Wake up? I should be the one telling you to wake up, disturbing Mr. Wheeler's donkey with your snoring. Poor donkey!"

Suhcrom rubbed his eyes. He couldn't believe he had fallen asleep on the back of Mr. Wheeler's cart. The yellowish-brown peel of his half-eaten banana hung limply over his hand.

He glanced around and recognized some of the

houses. As the cart approached the road that led to Palmerston Close, Mr. Wheeler instructed Naddih to pull firmly on the reins to bring the donkey to a stop.

"Whoa, slow down Miss Jawbreaker, slow down," Naddih hollered. *"She nah listen to mi, Mista Wheeler. Mi seh slow down, man...mi mean woman."*

"Let me have the straps, Naddih," said Mr. Wheeler.

"That Miss Jawbreaker is one stubborn donkey."

When Mr. Wheeler brought the cart to a halt, some of the mangos tumbled down and fell on Suhcrom. He picked them up and gently placed them back on the pile.

"Take some of those mangos to your father, Suhcrom. Take some ripe bananas, too."

Suhcrom and Naddih loaded their arms with fruit and jumped off the cart, thanking Mr. Wheeler for the ride. It had gone so quickly. As they headed down the road, Mr. Wheeler looked over his shoulder and waved goodbye.

"Have a good day, boys. And be sure to tell your father I said 'Howdy.'"

A big grin spread across Naddih's face. "That Mr. Wheeler is a nice chap."

It was getting late, so instead of going home first, they immediately went to the soccer field where Desreen, Muffet, Sterlin and Rodney were training with Nigel.

Their friends Hamburg, Mouse, Mikal and Amos had been there to watch and were hanging around, dribbling a soccer ball between them.

"Hey, everybody, look what Santa brought!" Naddih shouted as he ran towards his group of friends.

Everyone was happy to see Suhcrom and Naddih, their arms full of mangos and bananas. Even the grownups, who were there playing soccer, stopped their game and ran over to greet the boys.

"*Yu a no Santa Claus, Naddih. A weh yu big belly deh?*" laughed Rodney.

"Where did you get these fruits?" asked Hamburg as he took a banana.

"The Donkey Man."

"The Donkey Man?" Mikal asked, raising his eyebrow.

"Yes. Mr. Wheeler," said Naddih. "He told us to give them...." Before he could finish saying they were for his father, everyone grabbed a piece of fruit, and all he had left was his half-eaten banana.

"Don't worry, Naddih, let them have the fruits. I still have some for Jomfeh."

"Where's Nigel? How did training go?" asked Naddih.

"Training is over and Nigel went home. But he did ten laps around the soccer field," said Desreen. "He did great."

Naddih hooked his thumb through his belt loop. "Did he do any jumping jacks or cartwheels?"

"Yes, he did fifty jumping jacks, ten push-ups and five sit-ups. But I don't see why he would have to do cartwheels," said Desreen.

"Nigel fit, man. Him a go win di race!" Rodney exclaimed. He pulled a handkerchief from his pocket and started shining the spokes on Desreen's bike. "This bike is going to make Nigel famous. All of Jamaica is going to know about him!"

"Rodney, this isn't the bike Nigel is using tomorrow," Suhcrom said. "Well, at least I hope it's not this bike. We didn't find any handlebars or any other parts at the junk yard."

"Let's go to Mr. Burke's place now and see if he found any parts," suggested Sterlin.

When they arrived at the shop, they were surprised to see Mr. Burke polishing the new handlebars, putting the final touches on Nigel's bike.

"Wow!" they all shouted and cheered.

"Oh, hello there," Mr. Burke called out. "Hold on, I have one more thing to add before I'm finished." He went in the back room and came out with a flag—a pirate flag. It had a picture of a skull with a patch over one eye and a red rag on its head. "For good luck," he laughed.

Rodney got so excited that he started singing. "Nigel is going to win-win. Nigel is going to win-win."

Naddih joined in, picking up a metal rod and beating on an empty can. *Ding-ding.*

The whole group joined in with the singing, bobbing their heads, marching around in a circle and stomping their feet to the beat.

Nigel is going to win-win. Ding-ding. Nigel is going to win-win. Ding-ding. Win-win, ding-ding. Ding-ding, win-win. Nigel is going to win-win!

"Yippee!" Muffet shouted as she jumped with glee. Desreen giggled and gave her a big hug. Then they all laughed and gave each other "high fives."

Just then, Naddih noticed the reflector on the floor, the one he'd salvaged from the junk yard. It had fallen out of his pocket. He picked it up and handed it to Mr. Burke.

"Can you add one more thing please, Mr. Burke?" he asked. "Can you put this on the back wheel?"

"That's really nice," Mr. Burke replied with a smile. "Sure, I will put it on right now."

"Sterlin, should we pay Mr. Burke now?" Naddih whispered.

"Yes, but tell him that we're a dollar short," said Sterlin.

"Umm...Mr. Burke, we have good news and bad news," Naddih sighed. "Which one do you want to hear first?"

Suhcrom nudged Naddih's arm. "Stop your nonsense. Just say it."

"It's not nonsense. That's how grown-ups talk."

"Well, you're not a grown-up," Rodney laughed.

"The good news is we have two dollars and seventy-five cents from collecting bottles and cans plus the one-dollar bill Rodney found. The bad news is, Mr. Burke, we've been chased by wild dogs all day long—first at the swamp, and then at the car dump, where we got chased by a crazy dog who had a patch over his eye and his back legs were strapped to wheels."

Rodney tugged on Suhcrom's shirtsleeve. "Did that really happen?" he whispered. Suhcrom nodded and shuddered at the thought of being chased by a dog ever again.

"We're still a dollar short," said Sterlin, handing over the money.

They all stood silently. Their eyes widened as they watched Mr. Burke count out seven quarters, six dimes and eight nickels.

"Kids, this is not the amount we agreed upon," he said kindly. He paused as they all moaned and hung their heads. "However," he continued, "I will take this as full payment because you all took responsibility for breaking your friend's bike and have worked so hard to raise the money to fix it."

With a huge sigh of relief, they began to cheer and shout, singing together as they left Mr. Burke's place. Nigel's bike was finally fixed and it had turned out to be more amazing than they could have imagined. It was going to be the best bike in the race!

"Nigel is going to win-win. Nigel is going to win-win. DING-DING!"

CHAPTER 8

The Final Lap

"**A**ll competitors please report to the starting line."

The announcer's deep voice boomed over the loudspeaker. It was the day of the Annual Jubilee Bike Race, and excitement filled the air. Crowds of people came from all over St. Catherine Parish—Bridgeport, Portsmouth, Naggo Head, Newlands, Waterford—to attend this big event that was held every year in Portsmouth, near Palmerston Close.

Music from all of the favorite Reggae artists filtered over the speakers, creating a festive mood as friends and neighbors milled through the streets past the food vendors. The air was filled with the aroma of ackee and salt fish blended with the woody scent of roasted peanuts. Some vendors offered fried fish and dumpling while others sold bun and cheese and beef patty on coco bread.

The race would start at the road by Palmerston Close and follow the street in a big circle, passing the other neighborhoods and ending at the starting point.

All along the route, racers' families and friends were already lined up, mixed in with merchants peddling their trinkets, souvenirs, balloons and confetti.

A bright green and yellow banner hung across the street at the starting line. The children's race was scheduled first, and the adults' race would follow. It was a day-long event, the highlight of bike riders throughout the entire parish.

At the first announcement, packs of bikes with their young riders began to gather at the starting line. Nigel checked his bike over one last time. Although he was a good rider and had raced against other kids in the neighborhood, this was the first competitive race he had ever entered. He had shied away from competitions in the past for fear of coming in last.

"Nigel."

"Yes, Mom?"

"I know you wanted that new Jamaican Jet Street Racer Bike. You have been a good boy all year long, doing your chores and saving your allowance. Also, you have worked very hard, getting all 'A's' in school so you could enter the Cadet Program."

"Yes, Mom. So are you going to get me that bike?"

All of the kids had seen pictures of this bike in the magazines. It was sleek and fast — faster than any other bike! Some said it could out race a race car and could fly if you reached top speed. Nigel really wanted it.

"Well, I will get you that bike—if you finish in the top three."

Little did he know that his mom was going to buy the bike for him just for entering this race. She wanted him to overcome his fear of competitions, and at the same time, teach him that he could only be good at something if he was willing to take chances—and she believed he could win.

Nigel's entire family was there to cheer him on. Many of his friends had come, too. It was a non-stop stream of well-wishers. Desreen and the rest of the team had set up a table to give out water and her delicious cookies. Nigel's mother smiled and gave him a peck on the cheek while he chewed on one of Desreen's cookies.

"Come on, Mom, not in front of my friends...."

"You know, Nigel is definitely going to win now," said Rodney.

"Why do you say that?" asked Suhcrom.

"Because his mom just kissed his cheek. That's good luck. He should let her kiss the other cheek!"

"Oh, be quiet Rodney. Did you let Mom kiss your cheek before you left the house this morning?" Sterlin laughed.

"No, why should she kiss me? I'm not the one racing."

"Ah, you're such a Mama's boy," teased Naddih.

"Naddih, leave Rodney alone. You're a Mama's boy, too," said Suhcrom.

"Guys, it's almost time for the race to start," announced Desreen."

Suhcrom, Naddih and the rest of their team all huddled around Nigel. They patted him on the back, offering their words of encouragement with last-minute instructions.

"Just stay in the top three 'til the final lap, Nigel, and then make your move," said Rodney.

"And click into gear when you're close to the finish line," added Naddih.

"Naddih, his bike doesn't have gears," Sterlin chuckled.

"Well, pretend it does, Nigel, and then click it into first, second, third and then fifteenth gear!"

"Okay, guys, I better get going now," Nigel said nervously. "See you at the end!"

"No, we're going to see you the whole time, Nigel. We're not going to wait till the end," shouted Rodney.

"Rodney, that's not what he meant," said Naddih. *"Mi nah go keep explainin' every ting to yu."*

Nigel took one last gulp of water. He wiped his hands

on his lucky shirt, the one with the initials "JJSR" across the front and a picture of the Jamaican Jet Street Racer on the back. He had worn it hoping it would help him win! It was almost starting time so Desreen called the team to attention.

"Rodney, your job is to make sure Nigel gets water. Muffet and I will hand out cookies."

"Why can't I hand out the cookies?"

"Because you would eat them all and stuff your little belly," Naddih giggled.

"Naddih, you, Suhcrom, and Sterlin should be on standby if Nigel falls off his bike and needs a bandage."

"What is one bandage going to do? What if he hurts both of his arms and legs?"

"Well, that's all I have."

"Naddih, enough of the questions. We're just here to help Nigel," said Suhcrom.

A second announcement interrupted the Reggae music over the loudspeaker.

"Last call. All competitors must be at the starting line now."

Nigel took his place among the sea of boys and girls who were gathered at the starting line. He knew he was up against some other kids who could ride really well. He pulled his bike up next to Fletcher, a boy from

Waterford, and nodded a greeting. To Fletcher's right was Axel, a lad from Bridgeport. Axel had already won a race in his home town several weeks ago, and Fletcher had won the Jubilee race last year. So they were both very experienced riders. Delroy, the bad boy from the Box Juice Gang, was one of the surprise competitors. He slid into place at Nigel's left.

"Is that who I think it is?" Naddih pointed as he tapped Desreen's arm.

"Oh yeh, that is Delroy, and his buddy Calvin," replied Desreen. "Ah, what is he doing? Did you see that? Guys, did you see that? Delroy just stole the flag off the bike in front of him."

Desreen's icy glare could have bored a hole right straight through Delroy. He must have felt it, too, because his eyes met hers across the crowd. Desreen narrowed her eyes and tightened her jaw. She was about to rat him out when Delroy put the flag back, just as secretly as he had taken it.

Suhcrom shook his head. "That boy is nothing but trouble."

"Where is he? Where is he?" Rodney got on his tiptoes, straining to see over the crowd.

"He's right there. Next to Nigel. Wearing the bright red and orange shirt with caterpillars all over it."

"Is he talking to Nigel? What is he saying to him?" asked Rodney.

"We don't know, but he shouldn't be talking to him," said Sterlin.

"He's distracting him," said Suhcrom.

Naddih cupped his hands around his mouth and yelled as loud as he could. "Focus, Nigel, just focus on the race."

"Shh…the race is about to start," whispered Desreen.

"Nigel, do you want some more water?" Rodney called out quickly.

"Man, be quiet. He doesn't need any more water. His belly is going to burst with all the water you already gave him." Suhcrom laughed.

The announcer's deep voice boomed again over the loudspeaker. "Ladies and gentlemen, and anyone who is standing in the path of the racers, please move out of the way. The lady who is wearing the Humming Bird tee shirt and waving the Jamaican flag, please step onto the sidewalk. Thank you."

One of the grown-ups stood at the side of the road waving his shirt like a flag when the final call was declared. "On your mark…Get set…GO!"

The mass of young riders took off as the flag dropped. All of the bikers at the front picked up speed quickly.

Those farther back were bundled together and had to take it more slowly until the crowd thinned.

"Don't trip over that way, Nigel. Move the bike the other way," Naddih yelled from the sidelines.

Nigel finally freed himself from the tangle of the other bikers and pulled out ahead. He was off to a good start, and before he knew it, he was flying! The crowds roared. By the second lap, he was doing well and was in second place. His mother raised her hands, waved a handkerchief in the air, and cheered him on. "Go, Nigel, go!"

"He's a real thoroughbred," commented Naddih.

"Thoroughbred? He's not a horse," exclaimed Suhcrom.

"I know he's not a horse, but look how he's speeding around the track on his super bike!"

However, by the next lap, Nigel lost some ground. Axel and Fletcher pulled way ahead of him. Several others had too, including Delroy. The mood became tense among his team.

"Oh no, he's falling behind," Desreen moaned.

Nigel's team rallied around for their friend as he rounded the bend. "Ni-gel! Ni-gel! Ni-gel!" they shouted. "Come on Nigel, you can do it. You can do it!"

Spurred on by their energy, Nigel began to gain momentum. He peddled faster and faster, his face dripping with sweat, his shirt drenched. Before long, he moved back into third place.

"Get him some more water," said Suhcrom. "He needs water."

"Where is his water bottle?" Rodney shouted. "It was right here on the table. Where is it?"

"Just get him some water," Sterlin ordered. "Now."

Rodney searched the table again but found nothing. So he picked up the large jug of water they had kept for reserve. As Nigel made the next corner, passing all of his team members, Rodney stepped out and tossed the water from the jug, splashing it all over Nigel's face. Nigel gasped! Both the surprise and the force of it knocked him off-balance. The bike veered off the side of the roadway onto the gravel. His tires skid through the pebbles, the bike dipping so low to the ground that he nearly fell over. In desperation, he reached out his arm to catch himself.

"*Ahhhhh!*" they all gasped.

"Hang on, Nigel, hang on," Desreen yelled.

"Get back on the bike, man, hurry!" Suhcrom shouted.

"Rodney, why did you do that?" asked Naddih.

"I couldn't find his water bottle," Rodney whined. "You guys were putting too much pressure on me. I had to do it. I had to!"

Nigel didn't give up. His bike dragged through the dirt, but he quickly recovered his balance. Then he heard something snap. *Ping!* They all saw it as he took off—one of the spokes had popped off the wheel. There was nothing he could do. He had to keep going.

Nigel peddled as fast as he could to make up for lost time. The muscles in his legs burned as he blew past Delroy and pressed towards the final curve in the road. The end was in sight. It was getting closer and closer. He was neck and neck with Fletcher and Axel as they approached the finish line. With every ounce of strength he had, he pushed with all of his might and inched past the two riders just as they crossed the line.

"He did it, he did it!" Naddih shrieked. "He won!"

"YIPEE!" Muffet shouted.

People on the sidelines were up on their feet, jumping up and down, waving their arms, screaming and applauding as clouds of confetti rained over the racers.

Suhcrom, Naddih and the entire team charged through the crowds to congratulate Nigel. They chanted as his fans tossed him in the air and carried him off the track.

"Ni-gel, Ni-gel, Ni-gel, Ni-gel."

"You did it, Nigel," Desreen called out to him. "We're proud of you!"

"Thanks, guys," Nigel said, waving to them. A huge smile lit up his face as he tossed his pirate flag to Rodney. "I'll be getting my new bike soon!"

"Look at Nigel, flying through the air, like a real hero," exclaimed Naddih.

"You know what that reminds me of, Naddih?" said Suhcrom. "It reminds me of the cartoon, *Superman and His Amazing Friends*, when they saved the world!"

"Did we save the world, Suhcrom?"

"Well, maybe not the world, Naddih. But if we didn't work so hard to get Nigel's bike fixed, and get him ready for the race, he wouldn't be getting a brand new JJSR."

"So...are we superheroes?"

"Yes, Naddih, I guess we are!"

Patois Words and Phrases
(Presented in order of appearance by chapter)

Main Characters

Suhcrom – (SU crom)

Naddih – (NA dee)

Enomih – (ee NO mee)

Evrohl – (EV roll); also known as Jomfeh (JOM fay)

Sterlin – (STER lin)

Rodney – (ROD nee)

Desreen – (DEZ reen)

Muffet – (MUF it)

Nigel – (NAI jel)

Chapter 1—Blast Off!

7 *A weh yu a give me alla dem checks fa?*—Why are you giving me all of those checks?

8 *bully beef sandwiches*—canned corned beef, chopped up and served between two slices of hard dough bread. Hard dough bread is much like a loaf of homemade bread with a firm crust on the outside and dense dough on the inside.

9 *Mi a di pilot, so wi a go av turbulence now.*—I am the pilot, so we're going to have turbulence now.

10 *Yu done mash-up wi gud spaceship. Wi dead now.*—You smashed up our good spaceship. We're dead now.

13 *Dats not di point. Yu early.*—That's not the point. You're early.

13 *callaloo*—A green leafy vegetable, similar to spinach or kale, used in popular Caribbean dishes.

14 *Yah mon*—literally means "Yes, man"; a very commonly used phrase in Jamaica, similar to saying "Okay, man."

16 *bulla cake*—Sometimes referred to as *bulla;* A rich Jamaican cake made with flour and molasses and spiced with ginger and nutmeg, usually eaten with cheese, butter or avocado. They are made into small, round flat loaves and are a traditional food of Jamaica.

Chapter 2—Flyin' Bike

21 *Likkle Wash-Belly*—a term of endearment typically used for the youngest child of the family

24 *Mikal, wi deh yah.*—Mikal, we're here.

27 *Yah mon, wi fool-fool eeh*—Yeh, man, we were foolish

29 *So dat no gud fi notin.*—So that's no good for nothing; or that's not good for anything.

30 *nunchuckles*—Rodney and Naddih's word for nunchucks

Chapter 3—Flyin' Bike—Take Two

33 *Mi know, mi know*—I know, I know

33 *Di names dem rhyme.*—Those names rhyme.

37 *Den how she a go learn fi talk gud if Desreen always a talk fi her?*—Then how is she going to learn to talk good if Desreen always talks for her?

41 *Dis nuh luk gud fi Rodney.*—This doesn't look good for Rodney.

42 *Yu tink him dead?*—Do you think he's dead?

42 *pump him leg*—A commonly used expression to describe the action of bending a person's leg up and down; believed to get the blood flowing; primarily used when someone gets hurt, and especially when hurt while playing soccer.

42 *Waata, waata, somebody get some waata.*—Water, water, somebody get some water.

42 *Wi out inna di field, man. Weh wi a go find waata out yah?*—We're out in the field, man. Where are we going to find water out here?

Chapter 4—What Can a Dollar Buy

48 *Nigel, yu hear mi a call yu name?*—Nigel, do you hear me calling your name?

51 *A weh him a seh?*—What did he say?

54 *Mi so hungry, man.*—I'm so hungry, man.

55 *Unu no know notin 'bout flava.*—You don't know anything about flavor.

61 *Man, di dumplin' dem salty.*—Man, these dumplings are salty.

61 *But gud, Suhcrom. Mi belly full*—But good, Suhcrom. My belly's full.

61 *crocus bags*—very large sacks made of burlap cloth

Chapter 5—Bottles and Cans

63 *A weh unu a beat down mi door fa?*—Why are you beating my door down?

63 *Unu a police?*—Are you the police?

68 *Ooops...take dat outta mi ration.*—Ooops, take that out of my ration.

68 *Mi neva tell yu dat.*—I never told you that.

69 *Dats not di point.*—That's not the point.

74 *Him run gud and fast pon him foot dem.*—He runs good and fast on his feet.

74 *Like di people dem who go a foreign and run for Jamaica.* —Like the people who go to foreign countries and run for Jamaica.

Chapter 6—Junk Yard Disaster

80 *Dats jus people a labba labba dem mouth, man.* —That's just people talking nonsense, man.

80 *pickney* —children

84 *fool-fool* —foolish or stupid

84 *atrampolin* —Naddih's made up word for "adrenalin"

Chapter 7—Mr. Wheeler's Donkey Cart

87 *Mi tink it out fi kill wi today.* —I think it's out to kill us today.

87 *Why him jus a falla wi so?* —Why does he follow us so?

90 *It nuh mek nuh difference, Mista Wheeler. Dem both chew on grass.* —It doesn't make any difference, Mr. Wheeler. They both chew on grass.

92 *She nah listen to mi, Mista Wheeler.* —She's not listening to me, Mr. Wheeler.

92 *Mi seh slow down, man...mi mean woman.* —I said slow down, man...I mean woman.

93 *Yu a no Santa Claus, Naddih. A weh yu big belly deh?*—You're no Santa Claus. Where's your big belly?

94 *Nigel fit, man. Him a go win di race!*—Nigel's fit, man. He's going to win the race!

Chapter 8—The Final Lap

102 *Mi nah go keep explainin' every ting to yu.*—I'm not going to keep explaining everything to you.

About the Authors

Marcus E. Mohalland was born and raised in some of the poorest neighborhoods in Jamaica. Many of his own life experiences are recounted in this story. He obtained his Master's degree from Binghamton University and resides in Vestal, N.Y. "I have always desired to write about my life in a way that would encourage youth to enjoy their childhood, be grateful for what they have, and motivate them to achieve their greatest potential."

Janet L. Lewis Zelesnikar, was born and raised in Endicott, New York. She obtained her Bachelor's degree from Syracuse University and is a Registered Nurse. She lives in Endwell, N.Y. with her husband, John, and her best furry friend, Cudder. "Every child deserves to have fun as they grow and learn and should be encouraged to use their imagination. I was privileged to have such a childhood."

Visit our website at www.mohallandlewisllc.com to learn more about us and our company.

SILLY NOMADS SERIES

Vol. 1 Silly Nomads From Palmerston Close

Vol. 2 Silly Nomads Go Ninja Crazy

Vol. 3 Silly Nomads Jubilee Bike Race Heroes

STAY TUNED...

THERE'S MORE SILLY NOMADS

COMING SOON...

"WI SO SILLY, MAN!"

99848757R00065

Made in the USA
Columbia, SC
13 July 2018